A NEW ATTITUDE

Starring

SUNIL NEVLA

Written by Lisa Shea

Little, Brown and Company
New York Boston

Little, Brown and Company

Hachette Book Group
1290 Avenue of the Americas, New York, NY 10104
Visit us at lb-kids.com

Little, Brown and Company is a division of Hachette Book Group, Inc. The Little, Brown name and logo are trademarks of Hachette Book Group, Inc.

The publisher is not responsible for websites (or their content) that are not owned by the publisher.

First Edition: January 2017

ISBN's: 978-0-316-39525-0 (paperback); | 978-0-316-39526-7 (ebook)

Library of Congress Control Number: 2016949867

10 9 8 7 6 5 4 3 2 1

LSC-C

Printed in the United States of America

Dedicated to my three
favorite pets, Tippy, Gigi,
and Comet, with love.

CONTENTS

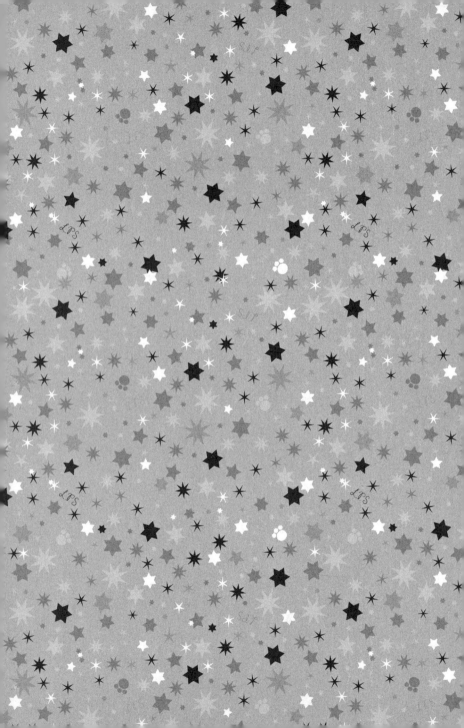

Chapter 1

"Only eight more days," Vinnie sang out.

"Only eight more days to what?" Zoe asked.

"Somebody's having a birthday," Vinnie answered with a huge grin.

"*Oooh!* Who?" Penny said.

All the pets looked at one another. Who was having a birthday?

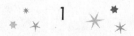

"Okay, who is it? Somebody say something," Pepper demanded.

Sunil blushed and put his head down. "It's really not a big deal," he said.

"Not a big deal?" Pepper yelled. "It's your birthday! It's an excuse for a party, and cake, and dancing, and celebrating! Your birthday is a HUGE deal. HUGE!"

"Oh yes, we'll have a fabulous party," Zoe said. "Sunil, I just need a little information from you, and I'll take care of the whole thing. Now, just tell me your favorite cake flavor, your favorite color, what kind of music you like—"

Zoe was interrupted by Blythe walking in with a pet carrier. "Attention, everyone," she said. "We have a new guest coming through. Ladies and gentlemen, allow me to introduce…" Blythe paused to reread the name tag. "Scarlett D. Panda."

"Another panda?" Penny squealed. She rushed over to be the first one to say hello.

Scarlett D. Panda walked out of the pet carrier calm, cool, and collected. "Hello, everyone," she said to the pets. "Scarlett's my name. It's nice to meet you all."

Scarlett was a red panda, and she was wearing a black-and-white polka-dot dress.

"I'm so happy to see another panda here!" Penny cried. She immediately gave Scarlett a big hug. "Hello, Scarlett. I'm Penny, and I just know you and I are going to be the best of friends."

Scarlett looked at Penny coolly. "Aren't you cute?" she said. "Thanks, Penny, but…just for the record…I'm not big on hugs."

"Oh, I'm sorry," Penny said, a little confused. "I just thought everybody liked hugs!"

Minka looked at Pepper, surprised. "Who doesn't like hugs?" she whispered.

Zoe was next to greet the new pet. "Scarlett, that dress is fabulous," Zoe gushed. She walked all around Scarlett so she could view her outfit from every angle.

"Why, thank you," Scarlett said. "It's just a little something I wore while filming a commercial in China. It was really great that we all got to keep our wardrobes."

"You filmed a commercial? In China?" Pepper was impressed. "Wow, ladies and gentlemen, we are in the presence of a real TV star!"

"You mean TV *and* movie star," Scarlett replied. "I've had quite a few bit parts in films, too. I've been to London, Paris, Rome…all the big international cities. I have some great stories I could tell you, if you're interested."

"Oh, we're interested!" Zoe said. "I'd love to hear all about your TV and movie roles. And all the great costumes you probably got to wear, too!"

"And I'd love some tips from you about being on TV," Pepper said. "I do stand-up comedy and dream about being discovered some day."

Vinnie noticed Sunil seemed to be hanging on Scarlett's every word. He walked over to his friend. "What do you think of the new panda?" he said. "Isn't she something?"

Sunil nodded in agreement. "It's amazing," he said. "She came into this room full of strangers and just took over the place, as if she had been here her entire life! She wasn't the least bit shy or nervous about meeting new people."

"That's true," Vinnie said. "And did you see the way she just shrugged Penny off? 'I'm not big on hugs,' she said. Who says stuff like that? Especially to someone you just met!"

"She's certainly very confident," Sunil said. "And I think that's a very admirable quality. I always get a little nervous around new people. I could never just walk into a room and start talking to everyone like that."

"Yeah, well, whatever. Enough about the new panda," Vinnie said. "Let's talk about something more important—your birthday! I still haven't gotten you a present yet!

You have a little time to give me some ideas.
What do you want?"

I want to be more like Scarlett D. Panda,
Sunil thought to himself. But he didn't say
this out loud. He just smiled and told Vinnie, "I'll get back to you on that."

The next day, Sunil approached Zoe. "I
need your help," he said.

"Of course!" Zoe replied. "You know I'd
do anything for you, Sunil. What's up?"

"I need a makeover," Sunil said. "Inside
and out."

"Inside and out?" Zoe repeated. "I'm
confused—what kind of makeover can you
do on the inside?"

"Instead of being quiet, shy Sunil, I want to be...cool! Brave! Outgoing! Confident! I don't just want a new look—I want a new outlook!"

"Hmm...well, I don't know how much I can help with your new *outlook*, but your new look is going to be a cinch. And it will be fun! *Oooh*, I just love makeovers!" Zoe sang out happily. She studied Sunil for a moment. She looked him over from head to toe. After a few minutes, she shouted, "I've got it!"

"Got what?" Sunil said, startled.

"Your new look—you can be a pirate!"

"A pirate?" Sunil said dubiously. "Um, I don't know, Zoe..."

"Why not?" Zoe said. "Pirates are cool, brave, confident...everything you said you want to be."

"I know that's what I said," Sunil answered. "But...that's not the look I want."

Zoe sighed. "Okay. That's too bad, though. I was so looking forward to seeing you in an eye patch," she said. "All right. Let me keep thinking."

A little while later, she shouted again. "Okay, *now* I've got it!" she yelled. "You can be a superhero!"

Sunil sighed. "Really, Zoe? A superhero?"

"Again, Sunil...brave, cool, confident. They are everything you want."

"And they're not real, and they wear capes and masks. Zoe, I'm not talking Halloween costumes here. I'm talking about my life. Seriously."

Zoe nodded. "Okay, Sunil. I'm sorry. I guess I went overboard. You know I have a flair for the dramatic! But I think I'm beginning to understand what you want. For real this time." Zoe started rummaging through a closet where Blythe kept clothes and costumes the pets wore in various shows and contests. After a few minutes, she smiled.

"Get ready, Sunil. It's time for a whole new you!"

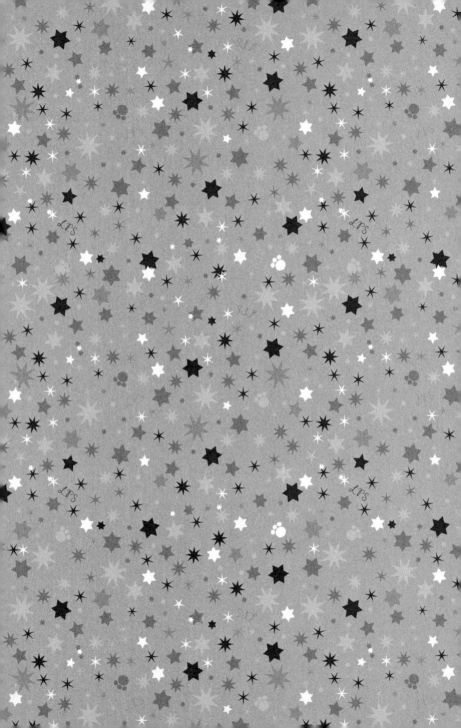

Chapter 2

The next morning, Blythe was setting out food for the pets. Most of them were huddled around Scarlett, who was telling them about the latest commercial she filmed.

"And then the announcer said, 'China... the most magical place on Earth,' and then there was a close-up of me chewing on some bamboo leaves," Scarlett was saying. "Later on, I heard it was the most successful travel ad for China the advertising agency had ever run!"

"Wow!" Vinnie said.

"That's awesome. You go, girl!" Pepper laughed.

"That's wonderful," Penny sighed. "I'd love to be a TV star."

"It might be fun to be famous for a little while," Russell said thoughtfully. "But I don't think I'd like it 24/7."

Scarlett stood up and struck a pose. "I've been famous, and I've been ordinary," she said. "And let me tell you, famous is better."

Minka pretended she was being swarmed by autograph hounds. "So sorry, I'm in a hurry," she said, waving her arms. "No autographs, please! Okay, for the paparazzi, maybe just one photo."

All the pets laughed, even Scarlett.

Blythe suddenly noticed Sunil and Zoe were missing.

"Where are Zoe and Sunil?" she asked. "It's not like them to be late for breakfast, especially Sunil."

Before any of the pets could answer, they heard Zoe's voice. "Attention, everyone!" Zoe said, and then she suddenly appeared from behind a curtain. "Ladies and gentlemen, I'm thrilled to present to you—the new Sunil Nevla! Everyone, put your paws together and give it up for the new Sunil!"

The pets (and Blythe) couldn't believe their eyes. In strolled Sunil in jeans and a white T-shirt, with a bandana wrapped around his head. "What's up, peeps?" he said. "Sunil Nevla is in da house. Whoop whoop!"

"*Whoop whoop*?" Vinnie said incredulously. He walked over to Sunil for a closer look. "Earth to Sunil. Hellll-ooo. What's going on? Is this some sort of a joke?"

Sunil looked at his best friend. "You of all people should know when I'm kidding and when I'm not," he said. "This is the new me."

Vinnie frowned. "What was wrong with the old you?"

Sunil sighed. "It wasn't that anything was wrong with the old me . . . It was just time for a change. Seeing Scarlett made me realize there were so many things that I wasn't, that I wanted to be. And these new clothes are just the beginning."

Minka jumped all around Sunil. "I like your new look," she said. "It's fun!"

"Well, you definitely look different, if

that's what you were going for," Pepper said. "So congrats!"

Sunil turned to Blythe. "Blythe, I notice you haven't said anything yet." Sunil did a little spin so Blythe could see his outfit from every angle. "What do you think?"

Blythe chose her words carefully. "I'm kind of in Vinnie's camp on this one, Sunil. I don't really understand why you want to change. But on the other hand, I will totally support you in your new look."

Sunil beamed. "Thanks, Blythe. That means a lot to me," he said.

Just then, Mrs. Twombly walked into the Pet Shop. She stopped dead in her tracks when she saw Sunil.

"Blythe! What have you dressed Sunil up as?"

Blythe was startled. Nobody in the world

knew that she could communicate with animals—not even Mrs. Twombly. She hesitated for a moment but then smiled. Why not just tell Mrs. Twombly the truth?

She looked Mrs. Twombly straight in the eyes and said, "Why, Mrs. Twombly, Sunil chose that outfit all by himself."

Sunil looked at Mrs. Twombly with a huge smile.

Mrs. Twombly laughed. "Oh, Blythe, you do have the biggest imagination of anyone I know…Well, at any rate, Sunil looks adorable. I'm going to straighten out the back room if anyone is looking for me. Have fun dressing up the pets!" she said, and Mrs. Twombly left, humming a happy tune.

Sunil's smile faded. "Adorable!" he fumed. "I look adorable?"

"What's the problem?" Zoe asked. "Adorable is good!"

"I'd kill for adorable," Vinnie agreed.

"Everyone wants to be adorable, Sunil," Minka said.

"Well, it's not for me," Sunil said. *Maybe I look adorable on the outside,* he thought. *But just wait until they see the new Sunil in action. Then they will change their tunes!*

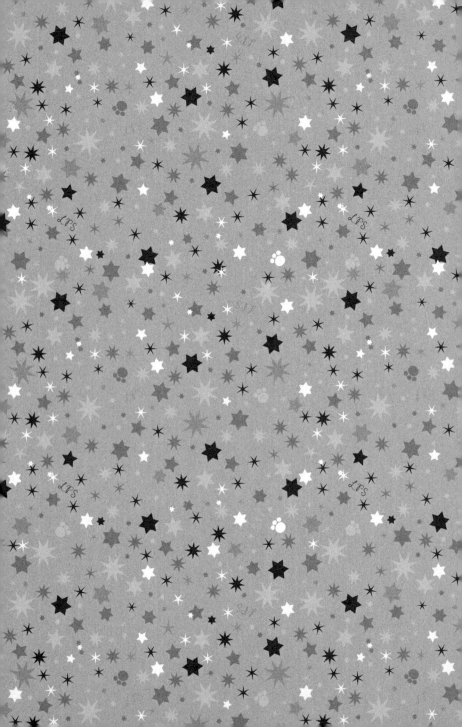

Chapter 3

It didn't take long for Sunil to start putting his new personality into action. The very next day, Zoe was complaining that she couldn't reach a top shelf where Blythe had stored a box of outfits she had designed for the pets. Zoe wanted to find a particular dress Blythe had made for her a while back. Ordinarily, Sunil would have just waited for someone else to help Zoe out. But Sunil realized this was a perfect way for the *new* Sunil to introduce himself to the pets. He marched over to Zoe and, without saying a word, lifted her high above his head.

"Sunil, what are you doing?" squealed Zoe. "Put me down!" But Sunil ignored her screams and walked her over to the shelf in question.

"Can you reach it now?" he asked.

"Oh! Yes!" Zoe said. She reached up and pulled down the box she wanted, and Sunil put her gently back on the ground.

"Thank you so much, Sunil," Zoe said, a bit dazed.

"Not a problem," Sunil answered coolly as he gave Zoe a big wink!

Zoe turned to Pepper with a big smile.

"You know, I think I'm liking this new Sunil," she said.

Sunil remembered how Scarlett chatted about her adventures and how the pets hung on her every word. He could tell about his adventures, too!

Before he talked to the group, Sunil went into the bathroom and practiced for a little bit in front of the mirror. He tried to look cool and relaxed. He imagined he was talking to a large group hanging on his every word. "Ah, yes, I remember that night when I amazed everyone with my magic. No one in the Pet Shop could figure out how I was able to guess their cards correctly every single time."

Then he imagined he was a movie star, being hounded for autographs. Just like Minka, he waved off an imaginary crowd.

"No, no, I'm sorry, no autographs today…
I'm running late. Thank you, thank you so
much!"

He left the bathroom and sauntered over
to where Scarlett was seated with Penny and
Vinnie. Sunil cleared his throat, and they
all looked up at him expectantly.

"Um…I was just remembering that
time I performed my magic act in front
of the entire Pet Shop…Remember that,
Vinnie?"

Vinnie stared at his friend, not sure
where he was going with this conversation. Of course he remembered. Everyone
remembered because they all had been
there. Except for Scarlett, of course. Wait—
was Sunil trying to impress Scarlett? Did he
like Scarlett?

If Sunil did like Scarlett, Vinnie wasn't going to let him down.

"Of course I remember," Vinnie said. He turned to Scarlett. "You should have seen him, Scarlett. Sunil was on fire! It was the most amazing magic act anyone had ever seen. People were talking about it for days...weeks even."

Scarlett turned to Sunil and gave him a small smile. "That's nice," she said. "I don't care much for magic tricks, though. However, when I was in London for a photo shoot, I did see some of the world's best magicians performing for the Queen."

Sunil's face fell. How could he compete with a story about a magician who met the Queen of England?

But Vinnie wasn't ready to give up. "Sunil

could compete with the best magicians in the world," he said proudly. "He's awesome. He just hasn't had a chance to perform for anyone important…yet!" He put an arm around Sunil. "My buddy will be famous one day…Just you wait and see!"

Sunil grinned at his buddy. "Thanks, pal!" he said.

At this point, Penny chimed in. "Sunil really is a great magician, Scarlett," she said. "I never know how he does any of his tricks!"

"Uh-huh," Scarlett said. Then she stretched and yawned. "Now if you guys will excuse me, there's a plate of bamboo leaves with my name on it…somewhere." And she left.

Vinnie turned to Sunil. "Don't worry,

buddy. By the time she leaves, Scarlett will be your biggest fan—just you wait and see."

"Huh?" Sunil said. "Um, okay? That would be nice, I guess."

Vinnie winked at his pal. "Your secret's safe with me," he whispered.

Sunil nodded, but inside he wondered, *What secret?*

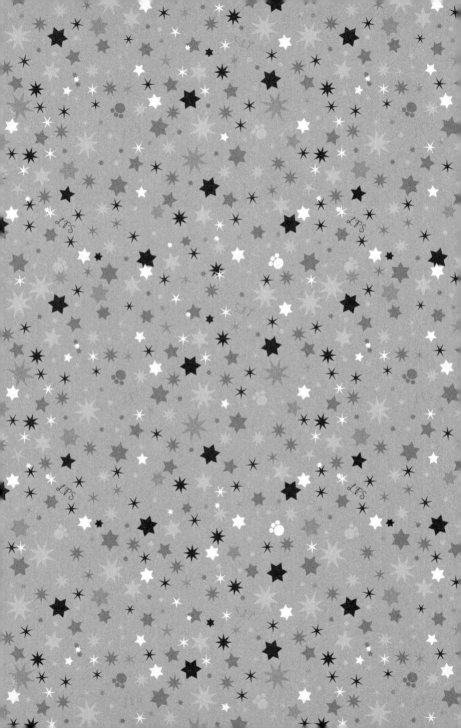

Chapter 4

The next day, all the pets were huddled together watching a scary movie. It was called *Night of the Living Pets*, and it was all about pets that turned into zombies!

Penny watched for about five minutes and ran out of the room, shrieking. But the rest of the pets watched the entire film. When it was over, Russell let out a low whistle. "Wow, that was creepy," he said. "It's going to take me a while to fall asleep tonight. I just hope that movie doesn't give me any nightmares."

"Me too," Pepper agreed. "I wish we didn't decide to watch that just before we went to sleep." She shuddered.

Russell stood up and started walking slowly toward Zoe with a glazed look on his face. "*Zooooooeeee,*" he groaned in a deep voice. "I've turned into a zombie hedgehog. *Zoooooooooeeee . . .*"

Zoe squealed, "Stop that, Russell! I know you're just kidding around, but you're still scaring me."

Russell didn't blink or crack a smile. He just kept walking slowly and murmuring "*Zooooooooooe . . . !*"

"All right, Russell, enough already," Pepper

said. "I know you're kidding, too, but it's late and you're kind of freaking me out."

"Me too!" Minka squeaked.

Suddenly, all the pets heard a noise in the back room.

Zoe looked at Pepper, her eyes wide.

"Did you hear that?"

Pepper nodded.

"It sounded like something creaking…" Russell said.

"And then there were footsteps," Minka whispered.

"Maybe…we should go check," Vinnie said.

"Who's *we*?" Scarlett asked. "Because *I'm* not going back there! If somebody comes here, I'm ready to fight, but I'm not going to go looking for trouble."

"Me neither!" Minka whispered.

Sunil took a deep breath. The old Sunil was timid, quiet, and shy. The new Sunil (he hoped) was brave and fearless. The new Sunil would never be afraid of a strange noise. He would jump at the chance to save his friends from danger. This was another perfect opportunity for the new Sunil to appear.

"No worries," Sunil said. "I'll go and check it out."

"Attaboy!" Russell said. "Go get 'em!"

Vinnie looked at Sunil in shock. He gulped. He realized he should probably help his buddy, even though he was scared out of his wits, too. "I'll come with you if you want," he said nervously.

"No," Sunil said firmly. "I need to do this alone."

"Good! I mean, okay," Vinnie said. "And

remember, I'm right here if you need me."

Wow, Vinnie thought to himself. *He must really want to impress Scarlett.*

Sunil took a deep breath and walked toward the back room. There were more rustling sounds. And more footsteps. *There's no such thing as zombies,* he told himself. *No such thing no such thing no such thing...*

He took another deep breath and switched on the light.

"Aaaagh!" he yelled.

"Aaaagh!" someone yelled back.

It was Penny!

"Penny!" he gasped. "What—what are you doing?"

Penny had her arms filled with snack bags. When she saw Sunil, she was so startled she dropped them all. But then she sighed and smiled happily.

"Oh, Sunil, it's just you!" she said. "I'm so glad you aren't a zombie! I didn't want to watch that scary movie, but I figured I'd surprise all of you with some snacks once it was all over. But then when the light suddenly turned on..."

Sunil laughed. "It's fine, Penny. I'm glad you weren't a zombie, too. Here, let me help you with those snacks."

Sunil helped Penny put all the snacks in little bowls on a serving tray. They then walked out together.

"Anybody hungry?" Sunil said, offering the tray to each person.

Russell snorted. "So that's it? It was Penny?" he said. "*Oooh*, scary."

Pepper gave him a look. "It *could* have been a zombie," she said. "And I didn't see *you* rushing to protect us."

Minka agreed. "That was very brave of you, Sunil," she said.

Sunil shrugged. "It was nothing."

"Nothing!" Vinnie shouted. "That was awesome! You were brave! Fearless! Daring to go where none of us would." He shot a look at Scarlett to see if she was listening. She wasn't. She was busy studying her nails.

Vinnie went over to Sunil and whispered in his ear. "Good work, buddy. I think she's warming up to you."

Sunil looked at Vinnie confused. *Who* was he talking about?

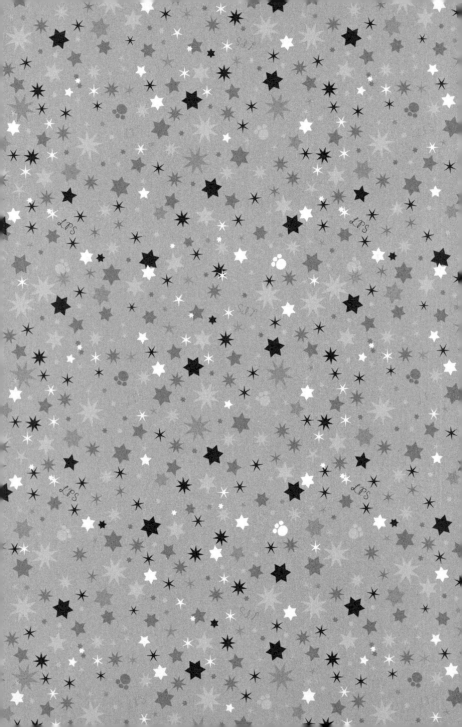

Chapter 5

The next day, Vinnie decided to do a bit of investigative reporting on his own. He waited until Scarlett was alone. She was texting someone on her phone.

"*Soooo*...Scarlett," Vinnie said, "who are you texting? Your boyfriend?"

Scarlett didn't even look up. "No, my sister."

"Ah," Vinnie said.

Scarlett looked up.

"Ah...what?" she said.

"So...no boyfriend?"

Scarlett sighed. "Not that it's any business of yours...no, I don't happen to be seeing anyone at the present time. Why?"

Vinnie shrugged. "Just curious. A pretty panda like you...I'm surprised you're not dating anyone."

"Well, it's just that I travel so much," Scarlett said. "It's hard to have a relationship,"

"It must get lonely, though," Vinnie said.

Scarlett put down her phone for a moment. She had a faraway look in her eyes. "You know, sometimes it does get lonely," she said. "I guess it would be nice to have someone special in my life, someone to talk to, share my secrets with..." Scarlett suddenly paused. "Hey, why all this interest in my love life all of a sudden?"

Vinnie shrugged again. "No special reason. Just making conversation. See ya." And he walked away, whistling a happy tune.

Scarlett watched him go. *I hope that gecko doesn't have a crush on me,* she thought. *He is so not my type.*

Scarlett walked back into the main room, where she found Zoe and Pepper bickering.

"What's going on?" she asked.

Zoe glared at Pepper. "She's making fun of my outfit. Again," Zoe said.

Pepper laughed. "Hey, I just said she was a little overdressed for a Tuesday afternoon. And she *is*!"

All the pets stared at Zoe. She was wearing a cotton-candy-pink tutu and a little tiara on her head.

"You know nothing about fashion," Zoe fumed.

"Yeah, well, I know enough that you shouldn't wear a tiara to dig a hole in the backyard," Pepper said.

"When was the last time you wore a tiara—ever?" Zoe snapped. "When did you ever wear anything that you couldn't find in the bottom of Blythe's scrap bag?"

"You're just a wannabe beauty queen!" Pepper said.

"You're a…wannabe anything!" Zoe shot back.

It was then that Sunil stepped in.

"Ladies, ladies, please! This is all just a huge misunderstanding. Pepper, we all know Zoe loves to dress up—whether it's a Tuesday afternoon or a Saturday night.

And she always looks lovely, wouldn't you agree?"

Grudgingly, Pepper nodded.

"And, Zoe...Pepper doesn't have your sense of style, but then again, who does? Yes, she always dresses casually, but that's her personal style, wouldn't you agree?"

"Yes..." Zoe said hesitatingly. "And... she may not always be wearing the height of fashion, but she always looks nice."

"There, you see?" Sunil said. "And if Pepper is able to accept the fact that you like to get dressed up, can't you accept the fact that she likes to be comfortable?"

"I suppose so," Zoe said. Then she laughed. "And I guess the tiara on a Tuesday is a bit much," she said as she took it off. "But it is *soooo* sparkly! I just love it!"

"I love it, too," Pepper confessed. "I think part of the reason I made fun of it was that I was a little bit jealous. I always wanted a tiara."

"Why didn't you say so?" Zoe said, and she gently put the tiara on Pepper's head. "Here, take this—I have plenty more!"

"Oh, Zoe, you're the best!" Pepper cried. "I feel just like a princess! Now you all have to excuse me for a moment, while I go look at myself in the mirror!" And with that, Pepper ran off.

Minka looked at Sunil admiringly. "Sunil, I never knew you were such a good problem solver," she said. "Zoe and Pepper were fighting for a good half hour before you showed up. None of us could get them to stop arguing."

Sunil grinned. "It's the new Sunil," he said happily.

Russell decided to have a chat with Blythe about the new Sunil.

"Blythe, aren't you concerned about Sunil?"

Blythe was surprised. "Not really. Why do you ask?"

"I just mean it seems pretty drastic. The new clothes…the new attitude, the whole 'new Sunil' thing."

"I think it's fine," Blythe said. "I wouldn't worry about it. I'm betting Sunil gets tired of this 'new Sunil' thing in a day or so, and everything will be back to normal."

"I hope so," Russell said. "New Sunil makes me nervous. I never know what he's going to do next. Old Sunil was nice and... predictable."

Blythe laughed. "I think that's the whole idea," she said. "To be unpredictable! I personally can't wait to see what the new Sunil does next."

Meanwhile, Vinnie decided that Sunil's romance needed a little push in the right direction. Later that afternoon, Pepper approached Scarlett with a box. It was a slightly lumpy package wrapped in brown paper. "Hey, Scarlett, I saw this package by the front door. Somebody must have left it for you."

Penny and Minka were curious, so they came over to see the package.

"Really?" Scarlett said. "I wasn't expecting anything." She tore off the brown paper and laughed. It was a plate of bamboo shoots! "Well, somebody knows what I like!" she said.

"Is there a card?" Pepper asked.

"Yeah, there is," Scarlett said. She read the card quickly and then said, "Ha! Listen to this: 'Scarlett, your fur is more beautiful than the reddest rose. I love the way your eyes sparkle and shine. And all I can do is hope and pray that someday you'll be mine.'" Scarlett turned the card over. "There's no name anywhere. It's anonymous."

"You have a secret admirer!" Penny swooned.

"That's so romantic!" Pepper said. "Who do you think it's from?"

Scarlett looked around the Pet Shop. "I'm not sure," she said. As she scanned the shop, her eyes fell on Vinnie, who was pretending to be busy eating a snack, but he was grinning from ear to ear.

"Like I said, I'm not sure," Scarlett repeated. "But I have an idea." *And I hope I'm wrong,* she thought to herself.

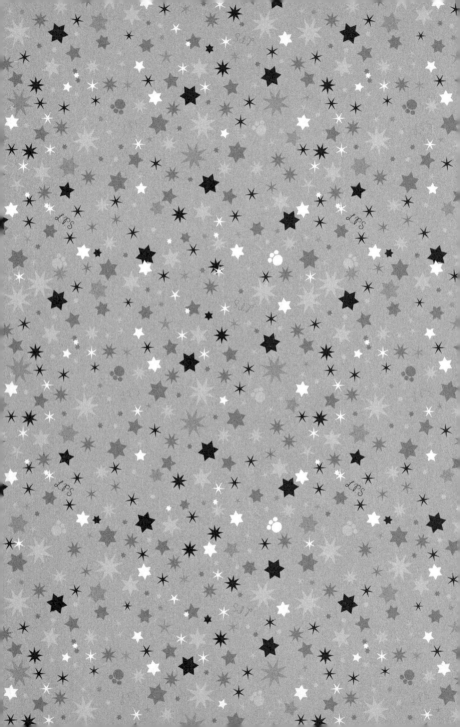

Chapter 6

After watching Scarlett open the package, Vinnie rushed over to where Sunil was practicing a card trick.

"Hey, Sunil!" Vinnie said. "Scarlett just got a gift and a romantic poem from a secret admirer," he said.

"That's nice," Sunil said.

Vinnie grinned and slapped Sunil hard on the back. "You're welcome," he said.

Sunil was confused. "You're welcome? What are you talking about?"

Vinnie grinned. "Just helping you out with your crush," he said. "It all makes sense now—'the new Sunil.' You, trying to be brave and charming…telling stories about your magic act and all that. Well, I just want you to know I'm here to help you in any way that I can, buddy." Vinnie paused. "Although I gotta tell you…I'm frankly a little surprised. Oh, don't get me wrong. Scarlett is definitely cute. But she's a little too tough for my taste…and I figured you'd feel the same way. But, hey, what do I know? And anyway, they say opposites attract."

Sunil took a deep breath. He didn't

want to get angry. But at the same time, he wanted to get his point across.

"Vinnie," he began. "Listen to me carefully. I. Am. Not. Interested. In. Scarlett. I don't know how you got that idea into your little green head, but believe me when I say I do NOT have a crush on her!"

Vinnie shook his head. "Which is exactly what a person with a secret crush would say! Dude, you don't have to be shy around me."

"I'm not being shy! I'm telling you the truth! I just wanted to try something different. For me! It has nothing to do with Scarlett…and get that silly grin off your face."

Vinnie just kept nodding and smiling as Sunil talked. He didn't believe a word of it. He knew Sunil was shy, and he was probably embarrassed that Vinnie had guessed his secret. But at the same time, he wanted

Sunil to know he would help him out any way he could.

"Okay, buddy. Sure. You don't like her. Fine. But just so you know...I'm here for you if you need me." Then Vinnie patted Sunil on the back again and walked away.

Sunil sighed. *Who knew trying on a new personality could be so complicated?* he thought.

A few minutes later, who should approach Sunil in the kitchen but Scarlett herself. She looked a little nervous and uncomfortable, which was unusual for her.

"Hey, Sunil?" Scarlett began. "Can I talk to you for a minute?"

Oh nooo! Sunil thought. *She must think I like her, too! She somehow figured out the secret admirer was supposed to be me! Or maybe Vinnie just decided to tell her.* Sunil didn't know what to do—all he knew was he did *not* want to have this conversation!

"Scarlett! Hey…what's up? Um, ordinarily I'd love to talk to you, but, um…I'm on my way to do something…something really important. Yeah, that's it! I have something really, really important to do right now, and it can't wait. So I can't stay and chat with you right now. Even though I would love to. But I can't. I gotta go. So…see ya." And Sunil dashed off so fast, he practically crashed into a wall.

Scarlett stared after him silently. *What a weirdo,* she thought to herself. No wonder he and Vinnie were friends. "They're like two wacky peas in a wackier pod," she said out loud. But she had to make sure Vinnie knew she wasn't interested in him! She decided to approach Sunil again later—after he finished doing his "really, really important thing." She groaned. Telling someone you're not interested was never easy. She wasn't looking forward to this task. At all!

Later that evening, Blythe carried a large cardboard box into the center of the Pet Shop.

"What's in the box?" Russell asked.

"I have a lot of leftover scraps of material," she told the pets. "So I thought it would be fun to make all of you some new outfits to wear on Sunil's birthday. Sunil gets to pick first of course." Blythe turned to face Sunil and was shocked at his appearance. He was wearing a sweatshirt with holes in it and a pair of jeans ripped at the knees.

"Sunil...is that you in there?" Blythe asked.

"Yes, it's me," Sunil said cheerfully.

"Oh...okay. It's just that you usually dress a little differently..." Blythe said. "You know...more conservative. Dapper. A dark sweater...a suit and top hat for your magic act."

"Ha! That was the *old* Sunil. This is the *new* Sunil, remember?" Russell explained, and he rolled his eyes.

"I saw that," Sunil said. "Sorry if you can't appreciate my new look."

"Sunil, I'll support you in whatever fashion you choose," Blythe told him. "It's just a little startling, you know?"

"It's fine, Blythe," Sunil said. "I understand." He peered into the box Blythe was holding. "Now, let's see what you've got in here." He rummaged around a bit and then pulled something out. "*Oooh!* Can you make me a pair of pants out of this, Blythe?"

Blythe gasped. "Sunil, that's a piece of black leather!"

"I know," Sunil said calmly. "Can you do it?"

"Of course I can do it," Blythe said. "But, Sunil…black leather pants? Seriously?"

"The new Sunil," Russell said, and he was about to roll his eyes again when Sunil yelled, "No more eye rolls!"

Blythe was totally baffled. What was going on here? What had happened to her sweet, shy Sunil?

Vinnie crept to Blythe's side. He tugged on her shirt so she would bend down to listen to him.

"He's doing it for a girl," Vinnie hissed.

"No, I'm NOT!" Sunil yelled.

But Blythe tended to believe Vinnie. He was Sunil's best friend, after all, and if Sunil was trying to impress a girl, this crazy new wardrobe made sense...sort of. Although she wished she could tell Sunil he looked fine just the way he normally dressed. But if he wanted to try something new, who was she to stop him?

"Okay, great," Blythe said. "One pair of leather pants, coming right up. Who's next?"

Sunil was wearing his new leather pants. He was sitting in Pawrista's, the new café in the Pet Shop. The café was crowded with people and their pets, and they were all staring at Sunil. "There he is—that's Sunil!" a French poodle cried. "He's so cool," another puppy agreed. A little girl pointed him out to her father. "Look, Daddy, look at that mongoose," she said. "Can we invite him to my birthday party next week? *Pleeease?*"

Sunil was beaming, basking in all the attention. This was everything he dreamed about!

"Wow, Sunil, you've certainly become popular," Pepper said. "It seems like everyone here is talking about you. All I keep hearing is 'Sunil, Sunil, SUNIL!'"

"SUNIL!"

Sunil sat up with a start. He had fallen asleep! Everything about Pawrista's had just been a dream.

"What were you dreaming about?" Pepper asked curiously. "You looked so happy! You had the biggest grin on your face."

"Oh...I was just dreaming about my birthday," Sunil fibbed. "I'm really looking forward to it."

"Really? The other day you didn't even want us to know it was your birthday. You told us it was no big deal," Pepper said.

Sunil shrugged. "That was then. This is now. And now I'm looking forward to it."

Pepper shook her head. "I don't know what to think. It's hard to keep up with you lately."

"Here's a good rule of thumb," Sunil suggested. "Just think of everything I used to do, and now think of the opposite."

"I'll try to remember that," Pepper said.

The next day, Penny, Minka, Pepper, and Zoe were trying to figure out what to get Sunil as a birthday gift. They all were a little confused as to what to get the new Sunil.

"This is tricky. What would the new Sunil like?" Minka wondered.

"That's easy," Pepper said. "Think of something the old Sunil would have liked, and then buy the opposite. That's what he told me himself."

"I must say, I kind of miss the old Sunil," Penny confessed. "The new Sunil asked me to go out dancing with him—at midnight! The old Sunil would never have done that! The old Sunil would bring me lemonade and tell me all about the latest book he's read. I miss that."

"I have to admit, I'm kind of missing the old Sunil, too," Zoe said. "At first, it was fun dressing him up in new outfits. But I thought after a day or two he'd get tired of it and want his old clothes back. Now he's always fighting me for my fashion magazines because he wants to make sure he's dressed in the latest styles! It's actually kind of annoying."

"I can understand wanting to be a little different," Pepper said. "It's why I like performing my comedy routines. I can be whoever I want to be onstage. But with Sunil, this is a little extreme. He's changing everything about himself—even the parts that people love about him. But what can we do? We can't just come out and tell him we hate the new Sunil! That would be mean, not to mention it would break his heart."

"Maybe he'll get sick of it on his own," Minka said. "Then we won't have to do anything. But in the meantime, we still have to think of a gift for him."

"If we were buying something for the old Sunil, it would be easy," Penny said. "Because I know the old Sunil would have liked *this*." She opened up a hobby magazine. "I saw this new magic kit and thought of Sunil right away. That is, the old Sunil. And I thought Blythe could make him a new magician's outfit. But now I don't know what he would like!" And with that, Penny burst into tears.

"Oh no, don't cry, Penny!" Pepper said. "You know what? Let's order that new magic kit. I have a feeling it's the perfect gift."

"And I'll tell Blythe to make Sunil a new magician's outfit," Zoe said.

"You never know…the new Sunil might change his mind…or maybe the new Sunil likes magic, too!" Pepper said.

Penny wiped her eyes. "That would be so great," she sniffled. "I just want to get Sunil something that will make him really happy."

"Then it's settled," Pepper said. "We buy the new Sunil an old Sunil present."

Just then Scarlett walked in. She saw all their serious faces, and Penny's red eyes from crying. *These pets are taking this birthday thing a little too far,* she thought. *It's up to me to set them all straight.*

"What are you all getting so worked up about?" she asked. "So you have to buy Sunil a birthday present. He either likes it or he doesn't. End of story."

"*Waaaah!* But what if he doesn't like it?"

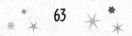

Penny wailed, and she started crying all over again.

Pepper looked from weepy Penny to bored Scarlett and back again.

"Are you sure you're both pandas?" she asked. "Because you don't seem like you're the same species...You don't even seem like you're from the same planet."

"What do you mean?" Penny said.

"Well, Penny, you cry at the drop of a hat. Scarlett...you seem like you've never shed a tear in your life."

Scarlett sniffed. "I cry...when it's something really sad. Not over something silly like a birthday gift."

"*Waaaah!*" Penny wailed again.

Chapter 7

The next day Blythe made new outfits
for all the pets for Sunil's birthday, as she
promised. She decided to go with a black-
and-white theme. She made four new
black-and-white polka-dot dresses for
Minka, Penny, Zoe, and Pepper that were
replicas of the designer dress Scarlett wore.

"Blythe, these dresses are fabulous,"

Zoe said, admiring herself in a mirror. "I don't think anyone could tell the difference between these dresses and Scarlett's dress, which probably cost hundreds of dollars."

"I could be on the cover of a magazine!" Pepper exclaimed.

"I love it, Blythe!" Penny said. "Thank you so much! You make the best outfits!"

"It's the prettiest dress I've ever owned," Minka agreed.

"You guys look fantastic, if I do say so myself," Blythe said. "Okay, the guys are up next!"

Blythe made Russell, Vinnie, and Sunil white shirts and black pants. And Sunil received the leather pants he requested.

"Blythe, these are great," Sunil gasped after he put the pants on. "But…are you sure they're supposed to be this tight?"

"Leather always fits snugly," Blythe said, trying to suppress a giggle. "Are you sure you want to wear those? I can always make you a plain pair of black pants like I did for Russell and Vinnie."

"Oh…no…these are fine," Sunil said as he slowly made his way to a chair. He wanted to make sure he could sit down! He sat down slowly and gently. *Whew! Made it,* he thought.

"Dude, you're not going to be able to eat your own birthday cake in those pants," Vinnie said. "Aren't you uncomfortable?"

"No! These are great—really!" Sunil said.

Pepper had to ask Sunil a question, and she was the bluntest of the group. "So, Sunil," she said, "I was wondering. Does the new Sunil still like magic?"

Sunil was quiet for a moment and slightly

panicky. He still loved magic—but was that not cool? Should the new Sunil not like magic?

Blythe noticed his hesitation.

"You know, Sunil, there are no such things as 'cool' activities and 'non-cool' activities," she said gently. "Whatever you like to do, and whatever makes you happy, is cool! That's how it works, just in case you were wondering."

Sunil smiled. "Thank you, Blythe!" he said. He turned to Pepper and said, "And in answer to your question, Pepper, the new Sunil loves magic—maybe even more than the old Sunil did."

"Good to know," Pepper said. "Thank you, Sunil." She looked at Penny and winked.

"Yaaay!" Penny cried, and everyone

turned to look at her. "Whoops!" she giggled. "Sorry!"

Vinnie went over to Scarlett and sat next to her. He thought this was another opportunity for him to put in a good word for Sunil.

"Sunil looks good in those leather pants, don't you think?" he said. "Maybe I should ask Blythe to make me a pair, too."

"Uh-huh. Whatever," Scarlett said. And she deliberately got up and walked away. She didn't want to give Vinnie any little bit of encouragement.

Vinnie watched her go. *Poor Sunil,* he thought. *He's going to have a rough time winning that one over.*

Sunil, meanwhile, was starting to feel pretty comfortable in his new persona. He was more outgoing, told more stories, laughed more, and even enjoyed being the center of attention once in a while. He was the first to volunteer for chores that involved heavy lifting, and the first to check out any other scary noises in the night.

"This is going to be the best birthday ever," Sunil told Vinnie. "As far as people giving me gifts—I don't want anything. I've already gotten everything I want."

"Well, almost everything," Vinnie said. "But don't worry—I'm still working on it."

Sunil groaned. "How many times do I have to tell you? I'm. Not. Interested. In. Scarlett. I'm not kidding, Vinnie."

"I hear you, buddy." Vinnie answered. "But what about what your heart says?"

"How can my heart say anything? I didn't even know it could speak," Sunil complained.

"Well, don't you worry, buddy," Vinnie

said. "Give me a little more time, and I'm sure she'll come around." Sunil suddenly remembered when Scarlett wanted to speak with him and he avoided her.

"You know, she wanted to talk with me the other day," Sunil said.

Vinnie clapped his hands together with glee. "I knew it! See, she is warming up to you! What did she want? What did you say?"

"I don't know," Sunil said. "I avoided speaking with her."

"You WHAT?" Vinnie cried. "What happened to the new Sunil? You know, calm, cool, collected, charming, great with the ladies..."

"Those are your words, not mine!" Sunil said. "I'm not any of those things...not yet, anyway."

"But, buddy, don't you see? She wants to

talk to you. She's warming up to you. She's finally coming around. How am I going to help you if you don't help yourself?" Vinnie asked.

"I don't need your help! I don't want your help!" Sunil said. "Why don't you just leave me alone?"

"Fine!" Vinnie shouted.

"Fine!" Sunil answered back as he stormed out of the room.

Boy, he really needs my help, Vinnie thought.

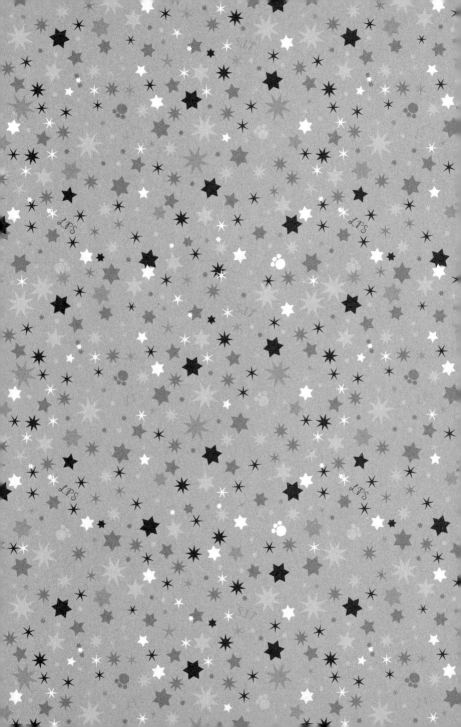

Chapter 8

Sunil decided to just avoid Vinnie for a while. *He's my best friend, but he's not going to bring me down or ruin anything,* he decided. He walked out into the kitchen area, where a few of the pets were eating. He saw Vinnie and hesitated for a moment. But then he realized it would be pretty difficult to ignore Vinnie. He just wouldn't start any conversations with him.

"Hello," he said to Vinnie.

"Hello," Vinnie answered back. Vinnie didn't want to stay mad at his friend, either. Sunil sat down at the table with the rest of the pets.

Everything was going fine until Pepper suddenly said, "Sunil, don't move."

"Why? What's wrong?" Sunil asked.

"Oh, it's no big deal. But there's a spider crawling right next to you. Stay still, and I'll—"

"A SPIDER?" Sunil shrieked. He jumped up on a chair. "Somebody get it, please!" he cried. "I hate spiders!"

"Sunil, chill," Vinnie said. "It's just a little spider."

"Vinnie, do something! Get it! Get it! Get it away from *meeee*!" Sunil yelled.

Pepper quickly rushed over and swatted

it with a newspaper. "No worries, it's gone," she said. "You can come down now, Sunil."

Sunil started to climb down, but then he hesitated.

"Really? Are you sure? It's really gone?" Sunil asked.

"Yes!" Pepper said, laughing. "Please, come down off the chair."

Sunil gingerly stepped down. He looked around at his friends. Nobody was looking at him. They all seemed to be avoiding him. Pepper's face was all scrunched up. Sunil could tell she was trying hard not to laugh. He glanced in Minka's direction. Minka tried not to giggle, but she couldn't help herself. Penny was trying so hard not to laugh, she was shaking all over! Sunil waited a couple of seconds, but then he started laughing, too.

"It's okay," he told his friends. "You can laugh. I guess it was kind of funny."

"I'm sorry, Sunil. I'm not trying to make fun of you, but the way you jumped up on that chair…It was just too funny!" Penny squealed.

"*Eeek! Eeek!* Is it gone?" Vinnie said, trying to imitate Sunil.

Pepper joined in. "Get it, get it, GET IT!" she said, also trying to imitate Sunil's voice. And then she started to giggle.

"Ha! Well, so much for Sunil the Brave," Sunil said ruefully. Then he burst out laughing, too.

Penny rushed over to Sunil and gave him a big hug. "Sunil, we love you no matter what," she said.

And even though Sunil was a little sad that he'd no longer be known as "Sunil the

Brave," he had to admit Penny's words made him feel pretty great.

The next day, Minka was up bright and early. She had several sheets of plain white paper spread out on the floor.

"Minka, what are you up to?" Blythe asked.

"Shhhh! Blythe, please be on the lookout for Sunil," Minka begged. "I'm going to paint him a special picture for his birthday."

"What a sweet idea!" Blythe said. "I'm sure he'll love that."

Just then Mrs. Twombly entered the shop. She looked at the sheets of paper and frowned.

"Blythe? What are all these sheets of

paper doing on the floor?" she asked. Blythe hesitated, then once again decided honesty was the best policy.

"Minka felt like painting," she said.

Mrs. Twombly's eyes widened, but then she laughed.

"Honestly, Blythe, that imagination of yours!" Then she studied Minka for a moment, who was holding a paintbrush and studying several different colors.

"Why, bless her heart, that sweet little monkey actually looks like she's really going to paint, doesn't she?" Mrs. Twombly cried. "Well, let her have her fun, but just don't get any paint on the wood floor," she said.

"I won't," Blythe promised. Once Mrs. Twombly was out of earshot, Blythe asked Minka, "So what are you going to paint?'

"I'm not sure yet," Minka said thoughtfully. "But I'm sure something will come to me if I think long enough."

Penny entered the room, carrying a box of her most colorful ribbons.

"Penny? What are you doing with all those ribbons?" Blythe asked her.

"I was thinking I'll perform a special ribbon dance for Sunil's birthday," Penny said. "What do you think of that?"

"I think that's a wonderful idea!" Blythe cheered.

"I just need to practice a little bit," Penny said. She pulled several ribbons out of the box and started twirling around. Blythe loved that all her pets were planning surprises for their friend.

"Make room people—pup with a package!" Zoe shouted.

Penny, Minka, and Blythe gathered around her curiously.

"What's in the box, Zoe?" Blythe asked.

"Oh, just a little something for Sunil," Zoe said. She opened the box and pulled out a beautiful silk top hat.

"I just thought he'd like a new magician's hat," Zoe said. "Especially since he's so... you know... *stylin'* now."

"It's perfect," Blythe said. "I know he's going to love it."

Just then Scarlett walked into the room. She took note of everything—Minka's painting, Penny's ribbons, Zoe's top hat gift.

"Geez, you people are sure making a fuss over Sunil's birthday," she said. "Why are you going to all this trouble? Just get a cake, slap a candle on it, sing happy birthday, and be done with it."

"A cake!" Blythe slapped her forehead dramatically. "I forgot all about getting Sunil a birthday cake!"

"Can't you bake one?" Penny asked.

"That's true," Blythe said. "I've baked cupcakes for the Pawrista's Café. How much harder can a cake be?"

"There you go!" Scarlett cheered. "By the way, have any of you seen the soon-to-be birthday boy around?"

"You mean Sunil?" Blythe asked.

"Of course I mean Sunil," Scarlett snapped. "Where is he? I need to speak to him about his buddy Vinnie."

Zoe looked at Scarlett strangely and lifted an eyebrow. "I haven't seen him in a while," Zoe said. "But I'm sure he's around somewhere."

"Okay," Scarlett said. "Well, if you see him before I do, tell him I'm looking for him, will you?"

"Sure. You need to speak to Sunil about Vinnie. No worries, Scarlett, I'll give him the message," Zoe said.

"Thanks," Scarlett said, and left.

Once she was gone, Zoe whispered to Penny. She was practically shaking with excitement.

"Did you hear that?"

Penny was confused. "Yes…she's looking for Sunil. So what?"

Zoe sighed. "Didn't you hear what she said? She was looking for *Sunil* because she needed to talk to him about *Vinnie*!"

"So?" Penny said. "I still don't get it. What are you so excited about, Zoe?"

"Don't you see?" Zoe cried loudly. "Read between the lines! It's so obvious! Scarlett has a crush on Vinnie!"

Chapter 9

Zoe decided she would play matchmaker. She went off in search of Vinnie. She found him using Blythe's laptop. Zoe peeked at what was on the computer screen. He was doing a search "What do pandas do for fun?" Aha! He liked Scarlett, too! It was perfect! *This is going to be easier than I thought,* Zoe thought to herself.

"Hey, Vinnie, what's up?" Zoe said.

"Not much," Vinnie answered, never taking his eyes off the screen. "What can I do for you?"

"Oh, nothing, I just felt like chatting," Zoe replied. "*Sooo*... I think Scarlett is leaving in a couple of days. That's sad, huh?"

"Yeah, it is," Vinnie agreed. "I really didn't have enough time to—I mean, we didn't have enough time to really get to know her, you know?"

"I do," Zoe said. "But you shouldn't worry. I think a certain someone definitely made an impression on her, if you know what I mean." She gave Vinnie a big wink.

"Zoe...wait! You figured it out? You know what I've been doing?"

"Of course I did, and you don't have to worry. That's why I stopped by. I wanted to tell you. She just said she wanted to talk to Sunil—" But Vinnie didn't let her finish.

"Zoe, that is the best news!" Vinnie cried. "Thanks so much for letting me know! Now I need to find Sunil and talk to him before Scarlett gets to him first."

"You go, Vinnie!" Zoe cheered. And she watched as Vinnie raced off. *He sure looks happy,* Zoe thought to herself. *It's nice to have a little romance in the Pet Shop!*

In the meantime, Blythe was busy making a birthday cake for Sunil.

"He never told us what his favorite flavor was," she explained to Russell. "So I just decided to go with a magical theme." She proudly showed off a shiny gold cake, three layers high. "This is all edible gold frosting," she explained. "And look!" She held up a tiny statue of a magician pulling a rabbit out of a hat. "This is what I'm putting on top of the cake."

"It's great, Blythe," Russell said. "I'm sure Sunil will love it. That is, if you can get him out of his room."

"What do you mean?" Blythe asked.

"Well, he hasn't come out since he screamed at that spider the other day. He laughed like it was no big deal, but I think secretly he may be a little embarrassed."

"Oh no," Blythe sighed. "I was afraid something like this would happen. Sunil just tried to change too much all at once. I was worried that it might backfire on him. I think I need to give him a little pep talk."

Blythe found Sunil in his bed, but not asleep. He was staring up at the ceiling.

"Sunil? Everything okay?" Blythe asked.

Sunil let out a long sigh. "Not really," he said. He sat up and looked at Blythe sadly.

"I thought that I'd be happier as the new Sunil. But I'm not happier at all. If anything, I'm sadder because I feel like I'm letting people down."

"How so?" Blythe asked.

"I feel like I'm a fake," Sunil confessed. "Here I am trying to be Sunil the Brave, Sunil the Charming, and I see a little spider and go crazy with fear. Sunil the Phony is more like it."

"Oh, Sunil, you're being too hard on yourself," Blythe said. "Don't you realize nobody is perfect one hundred percent of the time! Everyone gets scared, everyone gets cranky, everyone makes mistakes. And anyway, it's the mistakes and mishaps that make people love you. Who wants to be around someone who's perfect all the time? Not me, that's for sure."

"You mean, I can still be the new Sunil if I wanted to—even though I screamed at the spider?"

"Of course! You can be whoever you want to be," Blythe said. "Although I have to admit, I kind of miss the old Sunil. I like the new Sunil, but I loved the old Sunil."

"You know what, Blythe? I kind of miss him, too."

"Well, there's no reason you can't bring him back," Blythe said. "You know—Sunil, the original—back and better than ever!"

Sunil smiled. "I like that…Vintage Sunil."

"Vintage Sunil," Blythe said. "Zoe will

love it!" Blythe leaned down and gave Sunil a hug. *Maybe this birthday will turn out okay after all,* Sunil thought.

Scarlett, meanwhile, was thinking about how the pets were preparing for Sunil's birthday. *Maybe I was wrong,* she thought. *Maybe I should think about others a little more instead of always just about myself.* Scarlett decided she wouldn't get Sunil a gift (she really didn't know him), but it wouldn't hurt to give him a birthday card.

A little while later, Penny noticed Scarlett writing a card.

"What's up, Scarlett?" she asked.

Scarlett gave a little sigh. "Well...all of you are making such a fuss over Sunil's birthday. I still don't really understand it…I never got the whole 'happy birthday' whoop-de-doo, but I guess I got sucked into it a little bit. I made him a card."

Penny was shocked. "You made Sunil a birthday card?"

Scarlett nodded. "That's okay, isn't it? Why are you looking at me like that?"

Penny hesitated. "Oh, no reason, really. I guess I'm just a little surprised."

Scarlett gave a little laugh. "You know what? So am I."

Oh no! Penny thought. *Scarlett likes Sunil! Poor Vinnie! He's going to be heartbroken.* Penny decided the best thing to do was to tell Vinnie right away, before his feelings got even deeper.

She found Vinnie watching TV. "Vinnie, I need to talk to you."

"Uh-huh," Vinnie said, never taking his eyes off the screen.

"Vinnie, please. It's important," Penny said urgently.

Vinnie sighed and turned to look at Penny, who was staring at him with big, sad eyes. "Penny!" he cried. "What's wrong?"

Penny's eyes filled with tears. "Oh, Vinnie, I really didn't want to be the one to tell you this...but...but..."

"But what?" Vinnie asked. "Penny, don't cry! Whatever it is, it will be fine. I promise. Just say it."

Penny took a deep breath. "I think Scarlett likes Sunil!" she said. *"Waaaaah!"* She couldn't help it—she felt so bad for Vinnie!

But to her shock (and relief!), Vinnie broke out in the hugest smile.

"You're not just saying that, are you, Penny?"

"N-n-no," she stammered. "I just saw her writing out a birthday card to him. She said she didn't want to at first, but she just got... sucked in."

"YES!" Vinnie shouted, and pumped his fist. "Penny, please, PLEASE don't cry! This is the best news ever!" And he gave Penny a big hug and practically danced down the hall.

Penny watched him in disbelief. *Poor, poor, Vinnie,* she thought. *Smiling even though his heart was breaking. Waaah!* It was just too sad.

Chapter 10

The big day was finally here! It was Sunil's birthday at long last. Sunil got up, looked at the leather pants, debated whether or not to put them on, and decided against it. No "new Sunil" he decided. He was going with vintage Sunil instead.

He yawned. He couldn't decide whether he was tired because he hadn't slept well, or maybe it was because trying out a new personality was so exhausting. Either way, he was going to be happy when his birthday was all over and done with.

He walked into the kitchen. It was filled with balloons, and a big banner that said HAPPY BIRTHDAY SUNIL! was hung over the kitchen table. All his friends were there, with big, happy grins on their faces.

"Happy birthday!" they shouted.

Penny ran up to Sunil and gave him a big hug. "Happy birthday, Sunil!" she cried. Then she stepped back. "Oh...I'm sorry. Maybe I should have asked you first." She gave Scarlett a quick look. "Not everyone likes hugs."

Sunil grinned. "Well, lucky for you, I'm someone who loves hugs," he told her, and he gave her a big hug back.

Then he looked up and saw hand-painted posters all over the walls. Bright, cheerful splashes of yellow and gold.

"I did those," Minka said proudly. "I painted stars for you because, you know, you love magic, and stars are magical—and easy to paint."

"They're amazing, Minka," Sunil said. "I couldn't think of a more beautiful thing for you to paint for me. Thank you." He turned around and looked at everyone. "Wow, and you all look so nice, too! You're all in fancy black-and-white outfits."

"Well, it's a big day, after all," Pepper said.

"We wanted to dress up, so Blythe made us special outfits for your birthday celebration," Penny said.

"Because you're such a special guy," Blythe said with a grin.

"Wait a minute," Russell said. "We never thought to ask—does the new Sunil like fancy clothes on his birthday? Or should we all have worn ripped jeans and T-shirts?"

"I love fancy clothes on my birthday," Sunil assured him. "And look at this cake! I've never seen a gold cake!" He touched it gently. "Is it real? Can we eat it?"

"Yes, of course," Blythe told him. "Let's all sing 'Happy Birthday,' and then let's dig in!" Blythe started to light candles on the cake, but Pepper stopped her.

"Okay, before we have Sunil's birthday cake, there's one question on all our minds, and nobody's saying it," Pepper said. "So I'm going to be the one to ask it."

Sunil was surprised. "Sure, Pepper, you can ask me anything," he said. "What do you want to know?"

"Are you sticking with your 'new Sunil' personality or going back to old Sunil?" Pepper said.

Sunil smiled. "I have to admit, being 'new Sunil' was fun for a little while," he admitted. "But after a few days, I felt like I was playing a part in a play. It wasn't me. It wasn't real. So to answer your question, I'm going back to 'old' Sunil. But if you don't mind, I prefer the word 'vintage.'"

"*Oooh*, vintage! I like that!" Zoe said.

Blythe grinned at Sunil. "Told ya," she said.

"I always loved the old—I mean the vintage Sunil," Penny said. "I'm glad he's back!"

Vinnie then stepped up. "Boy, am I glad to hear that," he said. "Because here is a little something I wrote for you." He took out a sheet of paper and began to read.

Sunil, you were never the bravest
    mongoose, it's true.
But no one ever had a better buddy than you.
You're quiet and smart and listen to what
    I have to say.
And we have the best time no matter what
    game we play.
You're funny and clever and can pull a
    rabbit out of a hat.
You don't like spiders—so what! *No one
    cares about that!*
You're honest and loyal, never fake,
    always real,
And so we all have to say, we love the old—I
    mean, VINTAGE—Sunil!

Everyone was quiet for a minute. And
then...

"Waaah!" wailed Penny.

"Penny, why are you crying?" Zoe asked.

"Because that was *soooo* beautiful! *Waaaah!*" Penny cried.

Zoe shook her head. "She cries when she's happy, she cries when she's sad... What are we going to do with this girl?"

"Never mind her—when are we going to cut the cake?" Russell asked.

"Right now!" Blythe said. "Right after we sing 'Happy Birthday.'"

After the pets sang "Happy Birthday" to Sunil, Blythe handed a knife to Sunil to make the first cut. "Although it's almost a shame to cut it up—it's such a beautiful cake," Sunil said.

Everyone was quiet for a little while enjoying their cake. Vinnie went and sat next to his friend.

"So this is a pretty great birthday, isn't

it?" he said. He slapped Sunil on the back. "And it's going to get even better."

"I don't see how that's possible," Sunil answered.

"Oh no?" Vinnie looked around. When he saw Scarlett he called out, "Hey, Scarlett? Don't you have something for Sunil?"

Scarlett looked confused for a moment and then said, "Oh yeah," and walked over with her card. "Happy birthday, Sunil," she said.

"Thanks, Scarlett," Sunil answered.

Vinnie laughed. "Geez, you're a cool one," he said. "I think I'm more excited than you are! Open it up, open it up!"

"Okay, okay," Sunil said. He opened the card and read it out loud. " 'Happy birthday, Sunil. I hope you have a great day. Scarlett.' "

"That's it?" Vinnie said. " 'Have a great day,' signed Scarlett?" He glared at her. "You couldn't even sign it 'love'?"

"Why should I sign it 'love'?" Scarlett asked. "I don't love Sunil." She turned to Sunil. "I mean, no offense, Sunil."

"None taken," Sunil said.

"Why should she sign a card to Sunil with love?" Zoe said. "After all, it's you she has a crush on, Vinnie!"

"What?" Vinnie said.

"What?" Sunil said.

"WHAT?" Scarlett yelled.

"You were saying you wanted to talk to Sunil about Vinnie," Zoe explained. "I figured it was because you liked Vinnie!"

"Please! I wanted to talk to Sunil about Vinnie because Vinnie had a crush on me," Scarlett explained. "And I wanted Sunil to tell him to back off because I figured Sunil could let him down easy."

"What?" Sunil said again.

"WHAT?" Vinnie roared.

"Well, you keep asking me questions like if I had a boyfriend, if you should get a pair of leather pants…you were always staring at me…what else should I think?"

"Hey, I was asking you all that for Sunil. Sunil is the one who's in love with you," Vinnie said.

"WHAT?" Sunil screamed.

"Come on, Sunil! The cat's out of the bag now," Vinnie said. "All this 'old Sunil, new Sunil, vintage Sunil' stuff. Look, it all started happening when Scarlett got here! Admit it—all of this was you trying to impress her, right?"

Sunil sighed. "Vinnie. I wasn't trying to

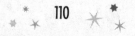

impress Scarlett. I was impressed *by* Scarlett. She just seemed so cool and confident all the time. I thought I wanted to be more like her."

"Wait a minute," Scarlett said. "So who sent me the mystery package with the bamboo shoots and the little poem?"

"That was from me," Vinnie admitted. "But I was sending them on Sunil's behalf because I thought he liked you."

"Wow...you're really a good friend. Well, thanks, Vinnie. The poem was cute, and the bamboo was delicious," Scarlett said.

"Don't mention it," Vinnie answered.

"Wait...so nobody is in love with anybody?" Zoe asked.

Sunil laughed. "I guess not," he said.

"Waaaaaah!" Penny cried.

"Penny, don't cry," Minka pleaded. "Here,

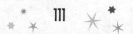

111

Sunil, open your presents," she said. "That will help cheer Penny up."

"Okay," Sunil agreed. He opened up Zoe's present first. "Hey! It's a cool new top hat!" He put it on immediately.

"Dashing!" Pepper said.

"Fabulous!" Zoe said.

"So vintage Sunil," Blythe agreed.

"And this one is from me and Penny," Pepper said as she handed him a beautifully wrapped package. Sunil opened it up and saw the new magic kit.

"Vintage Sunil loves magic!" he cried. "Thank you, Pepper and Penny! I can't wait to learn a new magic routine and amaze you all!"

Next, Blythe handed him a large box. "And this is from all of us," she said.

Sunil unwrapped the new magician's

outfit. He immediately put the jacket on. "It's perfect." He looked around the room. "I have the best friends in the entire world," he said earnestly. "Truly."

"Hey, how about showing me one of those famous magic tricks I've heard so much about?" Scarlett said.

"Yes, it's time for the Amazing Sunil!" Vinnie shouted.

"So, Scarlett. You want to see a magic trick. You mean like…this?" Sunil said, and in a blink of an eye, he pulled a rabbit out of his brand-new top hat! Scarlett was genuinely surprised. She really didn't think Sunil would be a good magician. She thought all the other pets were just saying he was out of loyalty to him.

"Hey, you know, that was actually pretty good," Scarlett said.

Sunil walked over and stood next to her. "Now pick a card, any card," he said.

Scarlett picked the two of hearts. Sunil told her to put it back in the deck, and then he asked Scarlett to shuffle the cards. She did and Sunil pulled out one card.

"Was your card the two of hearts?" he asked.

"Yes!" said Scarlett.

"Three cheers for the Amazing Vintage Sunil!" Minka sang out as all the pets applauded.

As everyone clapped and cheered for Sunil, Scarlett leaned over and whispered to Vinnie. "You know, he really is pretty cute. Do you think you can tell him I like him?"

Vinnie looked at Scarlett in shock.

"Wait. You mean you like him now? Seriously?"

Scarlett gave a little smile and nodded. "What can I say? I'm a sucker for a good magician," she said.

Vinnie put his head in his hands.

"Aaaagh!"

Sunil rushed to Vinnie's side.

"Vinnie, what is it? Is everything okay?" he asked.

Vinnie sighed. "Everything's just great. Happy birthday, Sunil," he said.

"Hooray for Sunil!" Pepper shouted, and all the pets cheered!

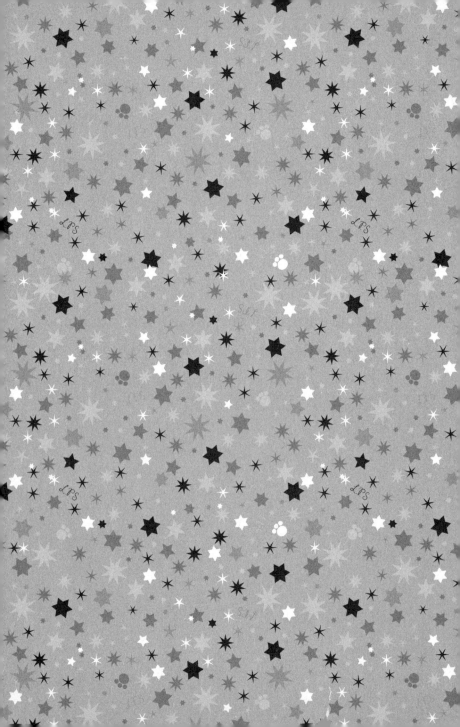

Turn the page for a look at

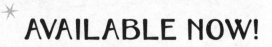

AVAILABLE NOW!

Chapter 1

Bzzz. Bzzz. Bzzz.

Blythe Baxter pulled the pillow over her head.

Bzzz. Bzzz. Bzzz.

What *was* that buzzing noise?

Bzzz. Bzzz. Bzzz.

It wasn't the alarm clock. Tomorrow was

Saturday; Blythe could sleep in as late as she wanted.

So what was it?

Eventually, Blythe couldn't ignore the noise any longer. She sat up in bed, rubbed her eyes, and turned on the light. That's when Blythe noticed her cell phone buzzing like crazy as it vibrated across her bedside table. The clock on her desk read 2:53 AM.

Who's calling me in the middle of the night? Blythe wondered sleepily as she reached for the phone. She pressed the answer button and mumbled, "Hello?"

"*Blythe*, darling, how *are* you?"

Blythe sat up straighter, completely wide awake. There was no mistaking that voice—it was the one and only Mona Autumn, publisher of the world-famous fashion magazine *Tres Blasé*. Mona was a glittering star in the fashion world, and Blythe had been in awe of her ever since Blythe sketched her very first fashion design.

Fashion wasn't Blythe's only passion, though. She also loved pets—all pets. And through the Littlest Pet Shop, Blythe was lucky enough to be able to combine both of her passions! Not only were Blythe's adorable and glamorous pet fashions for sale at the Littlest Pet Shop, Blythe also got to hang out with the wonderful pets who attended Day Camp there. The pets were always happy to model Blythe's latest designs, but more importantly, they were her friends.

Everybody knew that Blythe loved fashion, especially designing her own unique outfits. But what people *didn't* know was that Blythe had a top secret ability that she would never, ever reveal to anyone. Blythe could communicate with animals! At first, Blythe was incredibly freaked out by her unusual talent, but as she got used to it, Blythe started to understand just how amazing it was to understand animals, especially her pet friends. Not only could she help them when other people couldn't, but the pets could help Blythe whenever she needed them. She and the pets had had so many amazing adventures together—including a recent trip to the international Pet Fashion Expo, where Blythe and one of her pet pals, Russell the hedgehog, had been photographed for *Tres Blasé*! That was how Blythe had managed to meet someone as important and influential as Mona Autumn.

"I'm calling from Paris with the most fabulous news," Mona said briskly. "Are you sitting down, Blythe? Because you really should be sitting down."

Does lying down count? Blythe wondered. But before she could reply, Mona continued.

"Our latest issue of *Tres Blasé*—yes, that's right, the one with you and your prickly pet—has sold more than half a million copies!"

Blythe gasped. Half a million copies? That news wasn't just fantastic—it was amazing. Astonishing. Unbelievable!

"Half a million copies?" Blythe repeated, still in shock.

"And still selling! We simply can't print them fast enough!" Mona crowed. "Needless to say, *everyone's* thrilled. The fashion industry's thrilled. Our advertisers are thrilled. Even *I'm* thrilled—and I am *very* hard to thrill."

"I'm so—" Blythe started, but once more, Mona kept talking.

"And the public! The public is *beyond* thrilled! What they want, Blythe, is more. More Blythe Style, more fashion hedgehog, more *Tres Blasé*, more, more, more! And do you know what we're going to do?"

This time, Blythe didn't even try to answer.

"We're going to give it to them!" Mona answered her own question. "That's where you come in. We want you and Russell as the headline stars for a very special event being held in Paris in ten days!"

"A fashion show?" Blythe was so excited her voice sounded all squeaky.

"Better," Mona declared. "A fashion show at the first-ever Everyday Hero Awards, right on the runway at the Paris airport!"

Blythe gasped. "Mona, I'm honored," she said.

"Yes, of course you are," Mona replied. "This is big, Blythe. Really big. All eyes will be on you—which is what makes it so wonderful, since that means they'll also be on the everyday heroes who are being honored for their, well, heroics. Heroes get recognition, you get stardom, *Tres Blasé* gets to sell one *million* copies of our next issue. Everybody wins!"

Blythe grabbed her notebook and a pen. "Which fashions should I bring for the show?" she asked.

"Bring? No, no, no—you mean *design*," Mona corrected her. "We want all-new designs debuted here, Blythe. The public demands it. Now, for some direction: I want you to think *daring* and *dramatic* for your designs. Just like the heroes we'll be honoring."

Blythe wasn't sure she'd heard Mona correctly. "I'm sorry—did you say *all-new* designs?" she repeated. "For a show that's in *two weeks*?"

"Not two weeks. Ten days," Mona said. "But there's no need to panic, Blythe. I'm sure you can come up with at least seven new designs by then. After all, you're a *real* designer, aren't you?"

"Um, yes, of course," Blythe said, trying to sound confident. But inside, she was about ten seconds away from panicking! Mona was asking for a lot—especially considering that Blythe was also juggling school and her responsibilities at the Littlest Pet Shop. But Blythe didn't want to let Mona down—or blow this amazing opportunity.

"We're giving you a lot of control, Blythe," Mona told her. "Since you'll be the only designer for this show, you'll get to make all the big decisions—from sets and lights to models—"

Blythe perked up immediately. "You mean I can choose the pet models, all by myself?"

"Exactly," replied Mona.

Blythe wanted to cheer out loud, but instead she did a silent fist pump. Before the photo shoot, Blythe had told her pet pals that they could all be involved—but then Mona changed her mind. That's how Russell had become the star of the photo shoot. The other pets weren't too upset, but Blythe felt bad all the same. She finally had a chance to make it up to them.

"I've got to run, but I'll call back soon

to finalize all the details," Mona continued. "Be ready to *wow* me, Blythe! *Ciao!*"

And just like that, Blythe's phone went silent.

"Bye, Mona," Blythe whispered. She put her phone back on the bedside table but didn't turn off the light. Instead, Blythe reached for her sketchbook and her favorite colored pencils. She had an international fashion show to prepare for—in *only* ten days.

There wasn't a moment to lose!

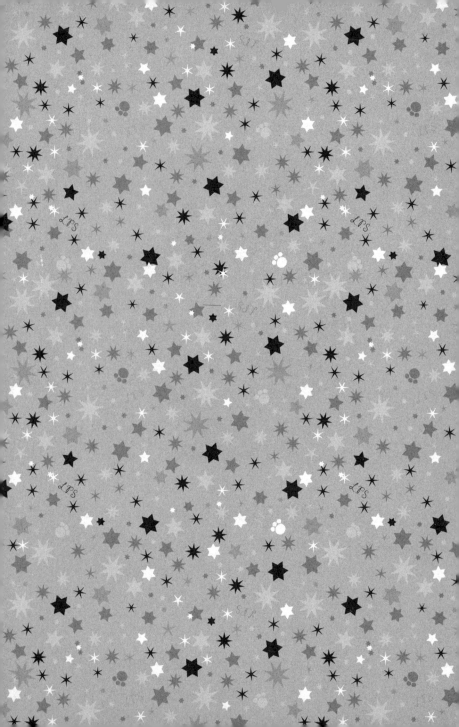

ON DVD 2/14!

Littlest Pet Shop

Pet Stars

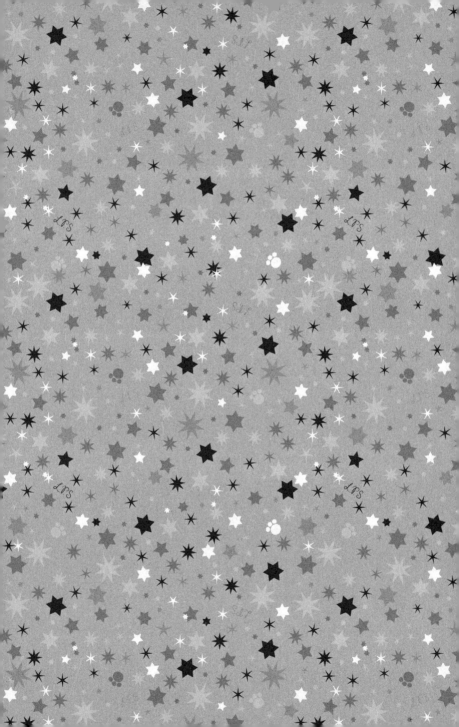

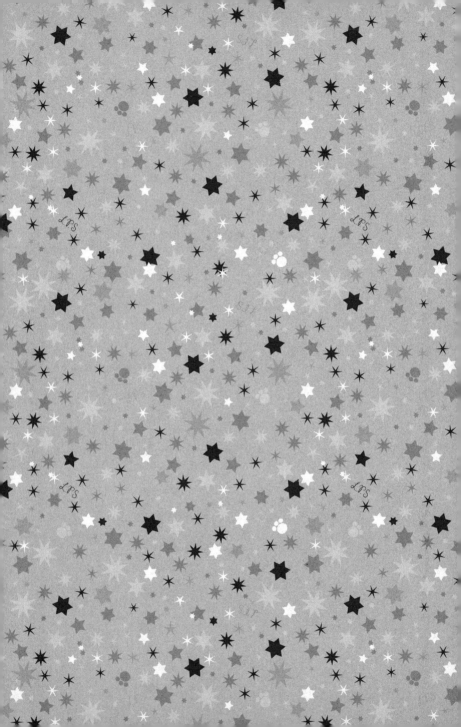